2/25

MY
BOOK OF
SECRET
STUFF

KEEP OUT

hinkler

This top secret book
is the property of

....

....

So keep out!

Congratulations!

You are now the lucky owner of your very own Book of Secret Stuff – a place where you can record everything from your secret nickname to the grossest thing you've ever eaten.

There are fun questions to answer, things to make and do, cool facts to absorb and blank pages to jot down things you see, do and think.

Use these top secret pages to record things that you don't want other people to know. There are pages to learn about being a secret agent and pages to record secret data. There are also lined and blank pages to record any other important, classified things.

And the best thing about this book is that you don't have to worry about what other people will think, because this is **YOUR** Book of Secret Stuff – a place where you can write things for your eyes only.

Use the invisible-ink pen if you want to keep something extra secret (it will only reveal what you've written when you shine the UV light on it).

You can also write secret messages by dipping the end of a pencil or a cotton bud in lemon juice and using that to write!

TOP SECRET

And don't worry.
This isn't a
journal, so you
don't have to
get all deep and
emotional if you
don't want to.
Just write and
have fun!

Personal stats

Stick a photo of
yourself here.

Mind your own business

Here is a secret place to record things about yourself that you don't want EVERYONE to know.

What is your family's embarrassing nickname for you?

....

....

....

What is your grossest habit? ....

....

....

....

Is there a silly thing you can do that you are secretly proud of? ...

....

....

....

....

....

My best friends are...

Stick a photo of you and your friends here.

Most awesome...

You must have done and seen some pretty awesome things in your time. Well here is a place to record what they are.

Film watched ....

Show on TV ....

Book read ....

Sports game watched ....

Computer game ....

Person ever met ....

Meal ever eaten ....

....

Comic read ....

Write about any other awesome thing you have seen or done.

....

....

....

....

Food file

The food I like best is

The food I eat most often is

The thing I most like eating for
breakfast is

The one thing I really hate eating is

The things my parents force me to eat are

One thing I pretend to like is

In secret, I sometimes eat

The grossest thing I have ever tried is

Spy club

Here are five steps to setting up your very own spy club.

1. Decide on a name for your spy club.

....

2. Recruit your most loyal and trustworthy friends.

3. Find a base for your spy meetings, and decide upon a password for admitting spy-club members.

4. Decide what your missions are going to be.

5. Write a list of your spy-club rules here.

....
....
....
....
....
....
....
....
....
....

Spy talk

Here are a few words that will help you sound like a spy.

- **agent** – person working for a spy group
- **asset** – a secret agent
- **babysitter** – bodyguard
- **blown** – discovered
- **case officer** – person who manages spies and runs operations
- **code** – secret language for writing confidential messages
- **cover** – pretend identity, or pretend reason for doing something
- **dead drop** – secret place to leave things
- **double agent** – agent working for two sides
- **ears only** – information that is too important to write down
- **handler** – person who manages other spies
- **mole** – secret agent that infiltrates another group or gang
- **shadowing** – secretly following
- **tail** – to follow someone
- **uncle** – spy headquarters

Freaky facts

Here are a few strange facts you can use to impress your friends and family.

- Nobody can lick his or her own elbow. Try it and see for yourself. Then have fun challenging your friends to lick their own elbows.

- Rabbits eat their own poop. Sounds gross but they do it to get every last bit of goodness out of the greens they eat.

- The Ancient Egyptians thought that you could cure toothache by killing a mouse and stuffing it in your mouth!

- The Ancient Romans wiped their bottoms with a sponge stuck on the end of a stick. And they shared it!

Uuugh! That's gross!

- The giraffe has such a long tongue that it can lick out its own ear. Yuck!

- No word in the English dictionary rhymes with orange. Ask a friend to think of one that does, and then wait...

Write your own freaky facts here:

Do you enjoy being scared? Complete this scary fact-finder.

What's the scariest...

Film you have ever seen? ....

....

Show on TV? ....

Book you have ever read? ....

....

Monster? ....

Thing you have ever done? ....

....

....

Thing you have ever seen? ....

....

....

Animal you can think of? ....

Dream you have had? ....

....

....

Fingerprints

Everyone's fingerprints are different, so they are the best way of identifying people.

They have been helping police to identify criminals for over 100 years.

There are three main types of fingerprint patterns.

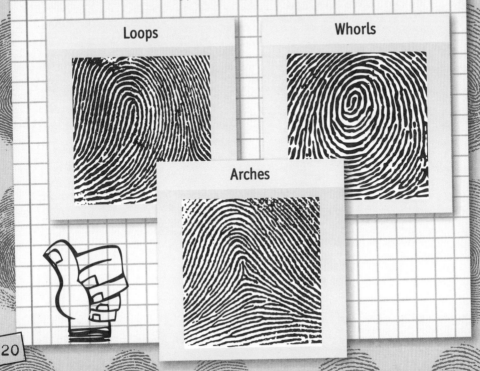

Loops

Whorls

Arches

Make your mark

- Take a pencil and scribble on a scrap of paper.
- Rub your finger over the scribble until it is covered with pencil.
- Take some sticky tape and press the sticky side onto your finger.
- Peel off the tape and stick it in the space below. Repeat for each finger.
- Take a close look at the patterns on your fingerprints, and compare them to the pictures on this page.

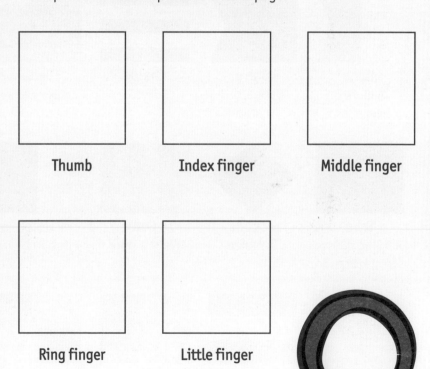

Thumb **Index finger** **Middle finger**

Ring finger **Little finger**

Flag codes

International code flags are sometimes used to send signals between ships at sea. They are great because they mean the same thing in all languages.

Alpha
Diver down
Keep clear

Bravo
Dangerous
cargo

Charlie
Yes

Delta
Keep clear

Echo
Altering course
to starboard

Foxtrot
Disabled

Golf
Want a pilot

Hotel
Pilot on board

India
Altering
course to port

Juliet
On fire
Keep clear

Kilo
Desire to
communicate

Lima
Stop instantly

Mike
I am stopped

November
No

Oscar
Man overboard

Papa
About to sail

Quebec
Request
pratique

Romeo

Sierra
Engines going
astern

Tango
Keep clear

Uniform
Standing into
danger

Victor
Require
assistance

Whisky
Require medical
assistance

X-ray
Stop your
intention

Yankee
Am dragging
anchor

Zulu
Require a tug

Why don't you make your own code flags and use them to send secret signals to your friends?

23

29

School file

What school do you go to? ....

What class are you in? ....

What lessons do you have? ....

....

....

....

....

Which is your favourite lesson? ....

Which lesson do you hate? ....

What is your best subject? ....

What is your worst subject? ....

Who is your favourite teacher? ....

Who is the school clown? ....

Who is the sports superstar? ....

Hobbies

What are your hobbies? ....

....

....

....

....

....

....

....

....

....

....

....

....

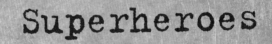

Superheroes

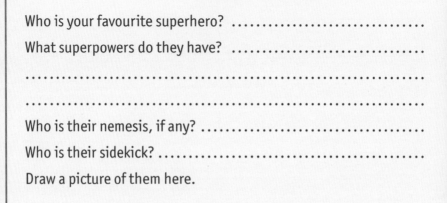

Who is your favourite superhero? ....

What superpowers do they have? ....

....

....

Who is their nemesis, if any? ....

Who is their sidekick? ....

Draw a picture of them here.

Super you

If you were a superhero, what would you be called? ....

....

What superpowers would you have? ....

....

....

Draw a picture of the costume you would like to wear.

Passing secrets

Codes are an excellent way of passing on secret messages.

Only the person writing the message and the person receiving it need to know the code.

TOP SECRET

One of the simplest codes to use is a shift code.

- To make a shift code calculator, you need to write two alphabets on two long strips of card.

- On one you need to add 5 extra letters on each end, as shown in the illustration.

- The lower card simply has to be shifted two or more letters backward or forward to get a new code.

| | | | | A | B | C | D | E | F | G | H | I | J | K | L | M | N | O | P | Q | R | S | T | U | V | W | X | Y | Z | | | |

| V | W | X | Y | Z | A | B | C | D | E | F | G | H | I | J | K | L | M | N | O | P | Q | R | S | T | U | V | W | X | Y | Z | A | B | C | D | E |

- Slide the bottom line forward or backward.

Write a secret message here.

Gaming

Most people love playing computer and console games, and we all have our favourites.

Make a list of your favourite games.

....

....

....

Which game do you like best? ....

Which one are you best at? ....

Keep a gaming diary here.

Date	Game played	For how long	Score, or level reached

Pranks

Sticky coin

- Put a little sticky tack on one side of a coin and stick it to the pavement.
- Find a hiding place and watch as people struggle to pick it up.

Eye-eye

- Use a pencil to blacken the eye rims on a pair of binoculars.
- Then get a friend to look through them.
- Try not to laugh too much when they look up with black rings around their eyes.

Wobbly egg

- Get an adult to help you make a small hole in each end of an egg.
- Hold the egg over a bowl and blow out the egg yolk and white.
- Carefully wash the egg, and then ask an adult to dry it in a warm oven for 10 minutes.
- While it is drying, make some jelly, using half the water suggested in the instructions.
- Then put sticky tape over one hole in the egg and place in an eggcup.
- Pour the jelly into the blown egg, and leave to set.
- Give a friend the 'hard boiled' egg, and watch them gasp as they peel it!

Gotcha

- Get a friend to ask their parents for a left-handed screwdriver.
- Sit back and watch them squirm when they realise that there is no such thing!

Pranksters' code of honour

- Never, ever play a prank that will hurt, or humiliate, anyone.
- Don't damage anything.
- Make sure everyone has a good laugh.

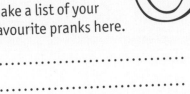

Make a list of your favourite pranks here.

....

....

....

....

....

....

....

....

....

....

....

....

....

Secret signals

Spies use signals as well as secret codes. Use these signals to pass on basic information to your friends.

- Stroking your left eyebrow means 'yes'.

- Stroking your right eyebrow means 'no'.

- Squeezing your nose means 'I understand'.

- Pulling your ear means 'I don't understand'.

- Touching the left side of your nose means 'go left'. Touching the right side of your nose means 'go right'. Touching the tip of your nose means 'go straight on'. All are useful when you are shadowing someone.

- Use whistles to warn your friends of something. One long whistle could mean 'watch out, someone's coming'. A series of short whistles could mean 'come here'. One really quick short whistle could mean 'run'.

Write some of your own secret signals here.

....

....

....

....

....

....

Big bang

Mix baking soda with vinegar for an explosive result.

You will need:
- baking soda
- food colour
- vinegar
- clear plastic container
- tray to catch everything that spills out

1. Pour a few drops of food colour into a glass or container, and then add a tablespoon of baking soda.

2. Pour in some vinegar.

3. Stand back and watch it bubble and fizz as it creates a chemical reaction. Awesome!

Make sure that you do this activity with your parents or guardians and stand safely back from the reaction.

Boredom busters

Here are 10 things to do when you are really bored.

1 Make up a song about being bored.

2 Practise making silly, sad, happy, angry, frightened and confused faces in the mirror.

3 Learn to play a tune with teaspoons.

4 Learn the capital of every country in the world.

5 Jump up and down and swing your arms around.

6 Write a secret message to your best friend.

7 Learn to balance a teaspoon on your nose. The trick is to secretly breathe into the bowl of the spoon.

8 Make silly animal shapes using your hands.

9 See if you can touch your nose with your tongue.

10 Write a list of all the exciting things you could be doing.

Just joking !!!

What do you get if you sit under a cow?
A pat on the head.

What do elves do after school?
Gnomework.

Student: Would you punish someone for something they didn't do?
Teacher: No.
Student: Good, because I didn't do my homework.

What has eyes but can't see?
A potato.

What do birds do on Halloween?
Go trick or tweeting.

What goes 'ha, ha, plop'?
Someone laughing their head off.

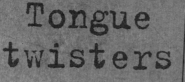

Tongue twisters

See how quickly you can say these tongue twisters without getting your tongue in a tangle.

Peter Piper picked a peck of pickled peppers.
A peck of pickled peppers Peter Piper picked.
If Peter Piper picked a peck of pickled peppers, where's the peck of pickled peppers Peter Piper picked?

She sells seashells on the seashore.
The shells that she sells are seashells, I'm sure.

One-one was a racehorse.
Two-two was one too.
One-one won one race.
Two-two won one too.

Yuck!

Here's a place to record all the things you really don't like.

Drink ....

Smell ....

Animal ....

Book ....

Film ....

TV show ....

Band ....

Song ....

Celebrity ....

Clothing ....

Others ....

....

....

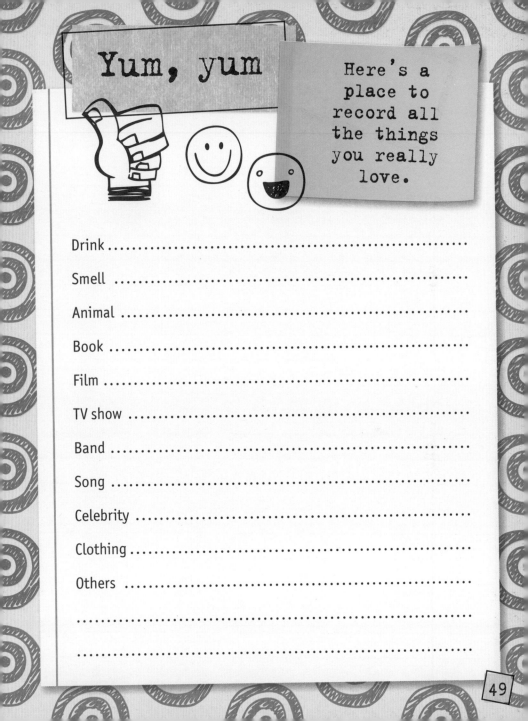

Yum, yum

Here's a place to record all the things you really love.

Drink ....

Smell ....

Animal ....

Book ....

Film ....

TV show ....

Band ....

Song ....

Celebrity ....

Clothing ....

Others ....

....

....

49

51

Scary monster

Invent your own scary monster.

Choose a name for your monster. ....
....

What does it do that is scary? ....
....
....

Draw a picture of your monster here.

Amazing growing finger

You don't need any props for this amazing hand trick.

1. Hold your middle and index fingers out in front of you, and pull the tips to the right, so that they look about the same length.

2. Tug on your second finger as if you are trying to stretch it.

3. Then hold the two fingers out again, but this time point them slightly to the left. The second finger will appear to have grown. Ta-da!

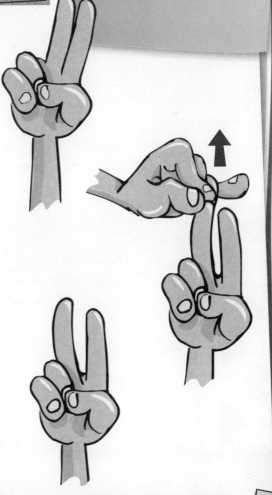

Morse code

- You can use Morse code to spell out a message with a mirror, using long flashes for dashes and short flashes for dots.

- Or you could use a whistle, using short blasts for dots and long blasts for dashes.

- You could also type these in dots and dashes

- Try using Morse code to spell out SOS (...___...), the standard international distress signal.

A .-	J .---	S ...
B -...	K -.-	T -
C -.-.	L .-..	U ..-
D -..	M --	V ...-
E .	N -.	W .--
F ..-.	O ---	X -..-
G --.	P .--.	Y -.--
H	Q --.-	Z --..
I ..	R .-.	

58

Write a message using Morse code.

0 -----	8 ---..
1 .----	9 ----.
2 ..---	
3 ...--	**Full stop**
4 ....-	.-.-.-
5	**Comma**
6 -....	--..--
7 --...	

Getting sporty

What is your favourite sport? ....

Do you play for a team? ....

If so, what is it called? ....

How often do you play? ....

What sport do you enjoy watching on TV? ....

....

....

Do you go and watch any sport live? ....

....

....

Who is your favourite sport star? ....

Who is your all-time sporting hero? ....

What is your sporting ambition? ....

....

....

Sports journal

Write about the best game ever!

Big adventures

Use these pages to write about any big ambitions, or great adventures you would like to have.

Perhaps you'd like to climb Mount Everest, explore the Amazon or take part in the Dakar Rally.

Bugtastic

Here are some cool facts you may not know about bugs.

Insects are the most numerous animals on the planet.

Ants can carry more than 50 times their own weight.

The tiny **mosquito** is the deadliest creature on the planet. When they bite people they can pass on malaria, which kills thousands of people each year.

The **Funnel-web spider** from Australia is one of the world's most deadly spiders. A single bite can kill a human within 40 minutes.

After eating, **houseflies** puke up their food and eat it again! Worth remembering when you see one sitting on your pizza.

Stink bugs give off a foul stench when they are frightened or crushed.

The **Goliath bird-eating spider** is the largest spider on the planet. It is about the size of a dinner plate.

Blow flies love feasting on animals – dead or alive. The female even lays her eggs in dead animals.

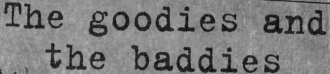

The goodies and the baddies

Some bugs are deadly, while others are pretty useful.

Top three goodies

1. Without the **honeybee** we wouldn't have a lot of the food we take for granted. They pollinate all sorts of plants – including cucumbers, watermelons, apples, and sunflowers. And on top of that they produce yummy honey.

2. It's thanks to the **dung beetle** that we don't have to wallow around in poop. They feed on animal dung and return the nutrients back into the ground.

3. The **witchetty grub** is eaten by some Australian Aborigines. It is highly nutritious and tastes like a cross between chicken and prawns.

Top three baddies

1. Mosquitoes are the most deadly creatures on the planet. These little blood-suckers are to blame for spreading all sorts of deadly diseases including malaria.

2. The **flea** is a tiny insect that feasts on the blood of humans and other mammals. They were responsible for spreading Bubonic Plague across Europe in the Middle Ages.

3. The **Japanese giant hornet** is enormous and fires flesh-melting venom, which can be deadly.

Record breakers

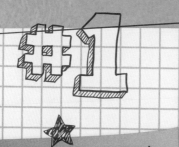

The centre of the **Sun** is the **hottest place** in the Solar System. No one has ever been there but it is estimated that it is a scorching 15,6000,000°C / 280800032°F.

Greenland is the **largest island** in the world. It covers an area about 2,175,000km2 / 836,109sq mi.

Oymyakon, in Russia, is the **coldest village** on Earth. It is so cold that it can take three days to dig a grave.

At 8,848m / 29,029ft, **Mount Everest**, in the Himalayas, is the **tallest mountain** in the world.

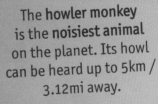

The **howler monkey** is the **noisiest animal** on the planet. Its howl can be heard up to 5km / 3.12mi away.

In 2006, veteran Star Trek actor William Shatner sold a kidney stone for $25,000, making it the **most expensive kidney stone** on the planet!

PBs

Use this space to record some of your personal bests (PBs). They can be anything from the farthest you have ever walked to the longest you have held your breath.

Best day ever

Record everything that happened on your best day ever.

Holidays

Keep a diary
of all those
important
school
holidays.

Use the following pages to keep a day-by-day record
of what you do in your school holidays.

Sweet treats

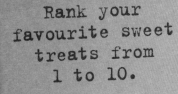

Rank your favourite sweet treats from 1 to 10.

1 ....

2 ....

3 ....

4 ....

5 ....

6 ....

7 ....

8 ....

9 ....

10 ....

Create your own sweet treat

Write about it here and draw a picture of it underneath.

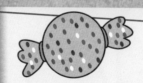

....
....
....
....
....
....
....

Random interrogation

Answer these questions as quickly and honestly as you can.

- What would you rather eat: chocolate or ice-cream?

....

- What would you rather be: a pirate or an astronaut?

....

- Would you rather lick a slug or eat dirt?

....

- Who would win if Wonder Woman and Superman met in combat?

....

- Who would you rather meet in a dark alley: Frankenstein's monster or Dracula?

....

- Would you rather hold a snake or stroke a tiger?

....

- Where would you rather go: into outer space or to the bottom of the ocean?

....

Going undercover

All good spies need to know how to disguise themselves, and lose someone in a crowd.

Quick disguise

- You can disguise yourself quickly by donning a hat and large sunglasses.

- Put on a wig or a fake moustache or beard.

- Hiding behind a newspaper is surprisingly effective.

- Walking differently than you usually do will help to confuse anyone looking out for you.

Losing a tail

- The first thing to remember when you think someone is following you is not to look behind you.

- Drop something and bend down to pick it up, so that you can subtly get a good look at whoever is following you.

- Wait for them to walk pass, and then head in the other direction.

- If they don't go past, take a sharp turn and head for the safety of an elevator or toilet.

- If there is nowhere to hide, try to lose your tail in a crowd.

Remember though, it's most important to be safe; if you're in danger head somewhere you can trust, like to your parents, teachers or the police.

Body language

It's amazing what people can tell you without actually speaking.

- A lowered head might mean someone is trying to hide something. It could also mean they are shy.

- A cocked head can mean someone is confused, or they are challenging you.

- Someone rubbing his or her hands together could be nervous.

- Clenched hands can mean someone is angry or nervous.

- Someone tapping his or her foot could be nervous, impatient, scared or excited.

- Crossed ankles mean that a person is feeling comfortable.

- If someone leans forward, they are interested in what you are saying.

- If a person mirrors your body language, it means they genuinely want to be your friend.

Your body language

Make a note of the body language you use, and what you think it means.

....

....

....

....

Time traveller

If you could go anywhere you wanted, including back in time, where would you go?

Perhaps you'd like to walk among the dinosaurs, meet up with the Romans or walk on the moon!

Draw a picture of where you want to go.

Top 3

Record your top three of the following things:

TV shows ....
....

Films ....
....

Songs ....
....

Bands ....
....

Video games ....
....

Comics...
....

Cars ....
....

Books ....
....

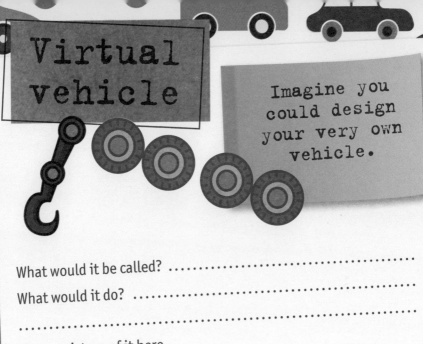

Virtual vehicle

Imagine you could design your very own vehicle.

What would it be called? ....

What would it do? ....

....

Draw a picture of it here.

Finding your way

The directions on a compass are called cardinal points. Here is a fun way of finding the cardinal points if you don't have a compass.

1. Find a stick and push it into the ground. Use a stone or stick to mark the spot where the tip of the shadow falls on the ground.

2. Wait for around three hours, and then mark the spot where the new shadow falls.

3. Draw a line between the tips. In the northern hemisphere, the first mark is west, and the second east. In the southern hemisphere it is the other way round.

4. To find north and south, simply draw a line at right angles to the first one.

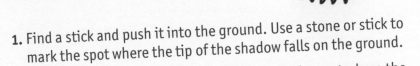

Get knotted

Use these diagrams to learn a few simple knots that will always come in handy.

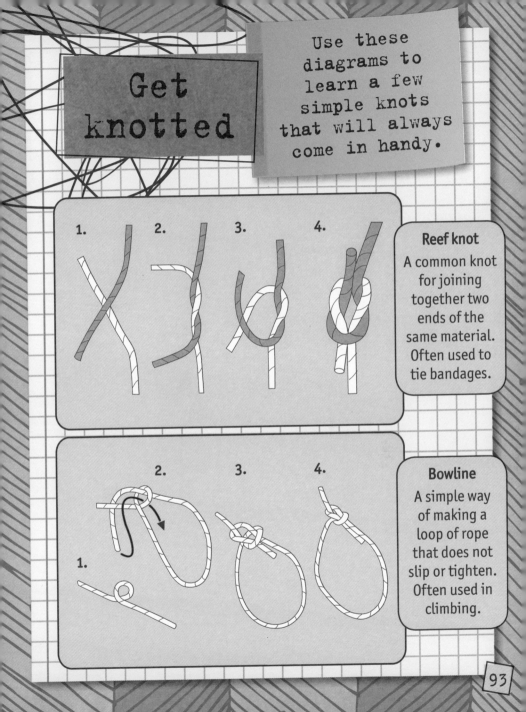

1. 2. 3. 4.

Reef knot

A common knot for joining together two ends of the same material. Often used to tie bandages.

1. 2. 3. 4.

Bowline

A simple way of making a loop of rope that does not slip or tighten. Often used in climbing.

Make your own lava lamp

You will need:
- A large, clean, clear plastic bottle
- A cup of water
- Vegetable oil
- Food colouring
- Fizzing tablets (such as Alka Seltzer)
- A plastic funnel

Make a cool lava lamp, using just four simple ingredients.

1. Pour the water into the plastic bottle.

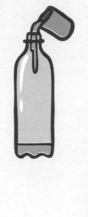

2. Using a funnel, slowly pour the vegetable oil into the bottle until it is almost full.

3. Wait for the oil and water to separate.

4. Add about 10 drops of food colouring to the bottle. Wait for them to mix with the water at the bottom of the bottle (DO NOT SHAKE THE BOTTLE).

5. Break a fizzing tablet in half, drop it into the bottle and let the madness begin!

Top Tips

• Try shining a flashlight through the bottle as it fizzes for an awesome effect.

• Experiment with different colours of food colouring.

New you

Close your eyes for a moment and imagine you could be anyone or anything you wanted for a day.

Who, or what, would you be? ....

Who, or where, would you visit? ....

What would you eat? ....

What would you wear? ....

Write a story about what you would do.

....

....

....

....

....

....

....

....

....

....